PEACEBOUND TRAINS

BY HAEMI BALGASSI

ILLUSTRATED BY CHRIS K. SOENTPIET

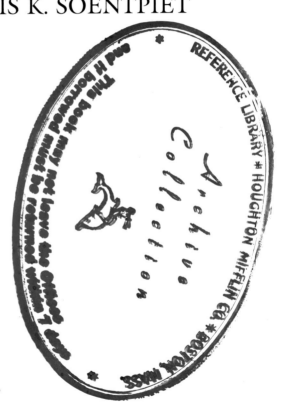

CLARION BOOKS/*New York*

Clarion Books
a Houghton Mifflin Company imprint
215 Park Avenue South, New York, NY 10003
Text copyright © 1996 by Haemi Balgassi
Illustrations copyright © 1996 by Chris K. Soentpiet

The illustrations for this book were executed in watercolor on Fabriano
watercolor paper.
The text is set in 14/18-point Galliard.

Printed in Singapore.

Library of Congress Cataloging-in-Publication Data

Balgassi, Haemi.
Peacebound trains / by Haemi Balgassi ; illustrated by Chris K. Soentpiet.
    p.   cm.
Summary: Sumi's grandmother tells the story of her family's escape from
Seoul during the war, while they watch the trains which will eventually bring
her mother back from army service.
ISBN 0-395-72093-1   PA ISBN 0-618-04030-7
[1. Railroads—Fiction. 2. Mothers and daughters—Fiction.
3. Grandmothers—Fiction. 4. Korea—Fiction. 5. Korean War,
1950–1953—Fiction.] I. Soentpiet, Chris K., ill. II. Title.
PZ7.B1976Pe   1996
[E]—dc20   94-26797
CIP
AC
TWP 10 9 8 7 6 5 4 3 2

I

ON CRISP BLUE DAYS, when clouds are high and few, I can see the trains cross the railroad bridge down in the valley.

If the wind is blowing east, I hear the whistle slice sharply through the air. *TWHOOOOOT, TWHOOOOOT!* The piercing song draws me to my favorite rock, eager to watch the train cars loop around the foot of Blossom Hill. I watch until the caboose disappears around the bend, and imagine the rest of the train's journey through other hill towns to the west.

I live with my grandmother up on East Blossom Hill. When my mother returns from the army this winter, she and I will live in town again, down in the valley. But for now, Harmuny's home is my home. Harmuny is the Korean word for grandmother.

One September day, I rush into the house to put my school books away, in a hurry to get to my rock. A train will be crossing the bridge at four o'clock. I don't want to miss it.

I am almost out the door when Harmuny calls out to me. "Sumi, there is a package from Umma."

A package from my mother! "What is it, Harmuny?" I feel a lump swell in my throat. Umma has been gone for months and months. We have never been apart for so long.

Harmuny hands me the plain brown box and says, "A gift, I would think. Have you forgotten that your birthday is only three days away?"

I take the box from her without a word, wishing I *could* forget my birthday this year. It won't be the same without Umma and her lopsided vanilla cake. Sitting on the edge of Harmuny's rocker, I tug at the tape and pry the box open. A rag doll tumbles out.

She has black yarn braids and chestnut button eyes, and I know that Umma made her to look like me. The red thread for the mouth is sewn higher on one side so her smile is crooked, like mine.

II

I DON'T WANT HARMUNY to see the sudden hot tears welling in my eyes, so I scoop up the doll and run out of the house, pounding the grass as hard as I can all the way to my favorite rock. There I sit, gulping in warm afternoon air, wishing Umma were here to wipe away my tears with a cool cloth.

I close my eyes and remember Umma's face: her smooth brown skin, her milk chocolate-colored eyes, the flowing ebony hair she sometimes let me braid.

The lump in my throat swells higher.

Last year, after Oppa died in a car accident, Umma found a job at an envelope factory two towns away. But she wasn't happy there. She worked long hours at night, so we hardly saw each other anymore. In bed, after Harmuny had tucked me in, I would cry myself to sleep, feeling as if I'd lost not only Oppa, but Umma, too.

When Umma decided to join the army last spring, she explained to me how important it was for her to go. The army would train her to be a soldier, and afterward pay for her college tuition. For the first time since Oppa died, Umma was excited about life again. I was excited, too. We dreamed about her studying to become a kindergarten teacher, or maybe a pediatric nurse.

But right now, I want her to be my mother and nothing else. I want her to be home, singing "Happy Birthday" to me in half Korean, half English. I long to hear her voice remind me to make a wish before I blow out my birthday candles.

Remembering the doll in my hands, I think about how she must have been in Umma's hands just days ago. My eyes still shut tight, I raise the doll to my nose and sniff for the scent of the lemony soap Umma uses. The yarn tickles my nose, but I don't smell anything.

III

I FEEL A COOL CLOTH ON MY FACE and open my eyes. For a brief moment my heart leaps, wishing for Umma, but it is Harmuny. She hesitates, then nudges me over on the rock and sits beside me.

"What are you doing out here, Sumi?" she asks, her voice kind.

"I'm waiting for the train to come." I point toward Blossom Hill and the railroad bridge.

For a fleeting second Harmuny's eyes cloud with distant memory. Then they clear, and she smiles. "I like to watch trains, too. I watch, and I remember."

There is something in Harmuny's voice that makes me wonder. Her eyes are half closed, and her lips are quivering ever so slightly. I can tell she is thinking about something important, something close to her heart.

"What do you remember, Harmuny?" I ask, sliding closer to her side.

Harmuny says nothing right away. Instead, she turns her coal-colored eyes toward Blossom Hill, and the skin on the bridge of her nose crinkles as her lips blossom into a tiny smile. When she speaks, her voice sounds smooth and young.

IV

"MANY DECADES AGO IN KOREA, long before I moved here to America, the world changed very quickly.

"I was married to your grandfather, your harabujy, whom you never knew. We lived in Seoul, in a neighborhood with many young families just like us. We had a son about your age, and a new baby girl—your umma." Harmuny pauses, her eyes far away again as she remembers.

"The Japanese were gone, and Korea belonged to Koreans again. Harabujy and I had hopes for a good life. Hopes for lasting peace.

"Then the wind changed abruptly, and the air rumbled with war. Koreans were fighting Koreans, brothers fighting brothers. There was nothing we could do to stop war from coming. Nothing. We felt helpless.

"At the very start, we tried to flee from Seoul. Harabujy gathered us into a truck and we set out to cross the great river. But the bridge was already down, destroyed by our military to keep enemy soldiers from crossing easily. We had no choice but to go back. A secret part of me was relieved . . . the part afraid to leave what I knew.

19

"Our capital city was quickly invaded by the North, and the growls of distant gunfire soon grew familiar. It chilled our hearts to hear it. The night skies were crimson from the bombs, and we passed many black hours crouched in the basement. When Seoul fell, only days into the war, we felt orphaned and dazed.

"That summer passed in a hazy blur. It was dangerous for men to be seen, so Harabujy hid in the basement during daylight hours. The children and I rarely went out onto the street. Fortunately, our neighborhood was in a remote part of the city, and our homes were spared.

"That September, when our allies forced the enemy troops out of the city, I was so grateful. United Nations soldiers came to protect us. Seoul was free again. But Harabujy felt our freedom would be temporary.

"'We must go soon,' he told me again and again. 'It is not safe this close to the North. We must make our way south, to Pusan.'

"But I was terrified. I did not want to leave our beautiful house behind, or my vegetable garden, or my mother's antique chests. We'd come this far, I thought; surely the worst was behind us now.

"Many of our friends were leaving. 'Come with us,' they said. 'It will be safe in Pusan.' But still we waited. For what, we never said. I spent the days praying for a miracle. At night I watched Harabujy pace the cold floor, his fists buried in his graying hair.

"Then one winter night Harabujy shook me awake. 'The Chinese are coming to help the North,' he told me in hushed tones. 'The U.N. soldiers will retreat, so we must go now, before it is too late.'

"We could not take much, only three bundles of the things we needed most. We had to leave everything else for the war to find. I thought my heart would break."

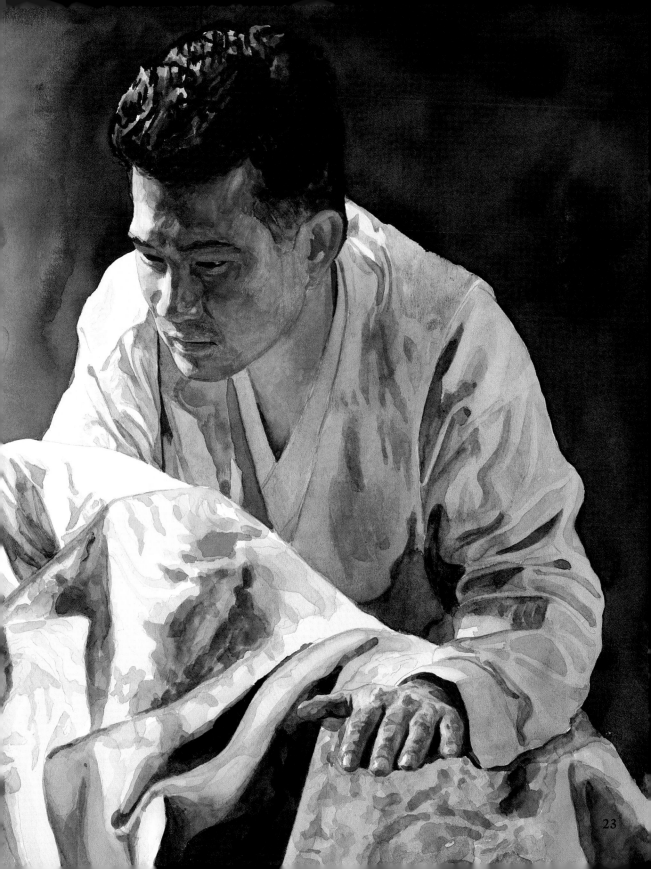

V

Harmuny stops then, and I see that she is crying. Gently, I take her hand in my own. It is trembling.

"What happened then, Harmuny?" I ask, trying to imagine her without the gray hair, without the wrinkles. I picture her as a young woman, a young mother, a young wife.

Harmuny breathes a hollow-sounding sigh. "Harabujy had arranged for us to cross the river by boat. We had to go before light, so no one would see. We walked briskly, through a chalky grayness cast over the woods by night's fading hours. Harabujy carried the two heaviest bundles. I held the small bundle in one hand, your uncle's hand in the other. A sling made out of my thickest apron wrapped your sleeping umma to my chest.

"We couldn't afford the risk or the energy to talk on the way. Only our shoes murmured soft shuffling words to the ground. Around us the night was still, except for the creaking of brittle tree branches stooped low with icicles.

"A fisherman was waiting for us in the shadows of the riverbank. His boat was behind him, and I remember thinking, *It looks so flimsy. Surely we will all be toppled by the river's current.* But to escape to the south, we had to cross the river. As Harabujy and the fisherman rowed, I fixed my eyes on the shifting sky and prayed that we would reach the other bank safely. Luck was with us that night, for we set foot on land soon after.

"Throughout the next days we continued our journey on foot. We saw many others doing the same. Some were riding ox carts. Others struggled to pedal rusted bicycles on harsh winter soil. Occasionally we saw a car or truck, but not often.

"Several times we saw military jeeps carrying fair-skinned soldiers. 'Americans,' Harabujy said. The colors of their eyes sparkled and swirled, like the marbles your young uncle left behind in Seoul.

"We heard about a train going south to Pusan. Harabujy was determined that we be on it. He feared there would be no more trains after this one. It could be our last chance for a safe passage.

"At last, on a frigid morning thick with fog, we glimpsed the looming shadow of the train ahead. As we drew closer, we could see people huddled alongside. So many people, thousands. Like us, they were dusty from travel by rural roads. Hungry babies wailed for their mothers' milk. Shivering children tugged on their mothers' and grandmothers' skirts. Everywhere I looked, a sea of grim, pained faces stared back.

"Suddenly, Harabujy turned to me, his face pale as the moon. 'Yuh-bo, you and the children must ride this train,' he said. His words clutched at my heart. 'What about you?' I demanded to know. And your uncle cried, 'Come with us, Oppa!'

"But Harabujy gripped my hand, so tightly that my knuckles ached, and said, 'I must go and do my part in this war, as a soldier. It is my duty, Yuh-bo.' If there had been more time, I would have argued with him further. But there was no time left."

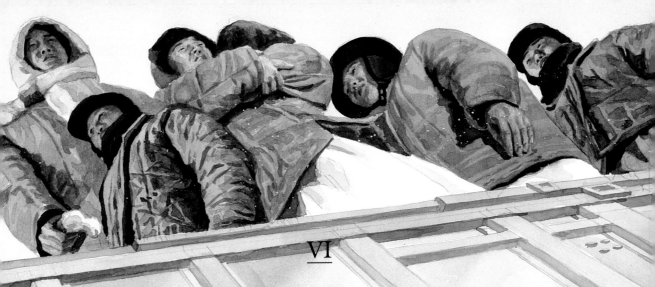

VI

Harmuny coughs and shudders, pulls on her shawl. Briskly she rubs her hands together and blows on them. When she speaks again, there is a new tremor in her voice.

"There was no more room inside the train. People were gasping for breath in the cars. Too many people. The only room left was on the roof, and that is where Harabujy put us.

"I thought he was crazy. 'How can we ride on the roof?' I wanted to know. But he was stubborn. 'You must ride this train,' he insisted again and again. 'If the roof will carry you safely to Pusan, it is where you must be.'

"I took your umma out of the apron sling and handed her to Harabujy, then somehow managed to climb up to the roof. I cannot remember now how I did it. Maybe there was a ladder on the side of the train; I do not know. Harabujy lifted your umma up to me, then her brother, your uncle. Many people were already there. Everyone was scrambling for room, wedging toward the center.

"Soon even the roof was filled, and I saw many people arriving late . . . too late to ride the train. The sun was rising, and the sky was now part blue, part rose. The fog had lifted. I thought, *How can this be happening on such a beautiful day?*"

Harmuny wipes her eyes, and I give her hand a squeeze. She finds my face through her tears and sweeps my bangs with fluttering fingers. She kisses my hand before continuing with her story.

"The train would depart soon, so we had only minutes for good-byes. I think now that this was good. A longer time would have been harder. I would have wept more.

"Harabujy embraced his son and daughter tightly, more tightly than I'd ever seen him do before. Then he held my hand to his cheek, blue with cold. We could not speak; there was too much emotion in both of us. We just tried to memorize each other's eyes.

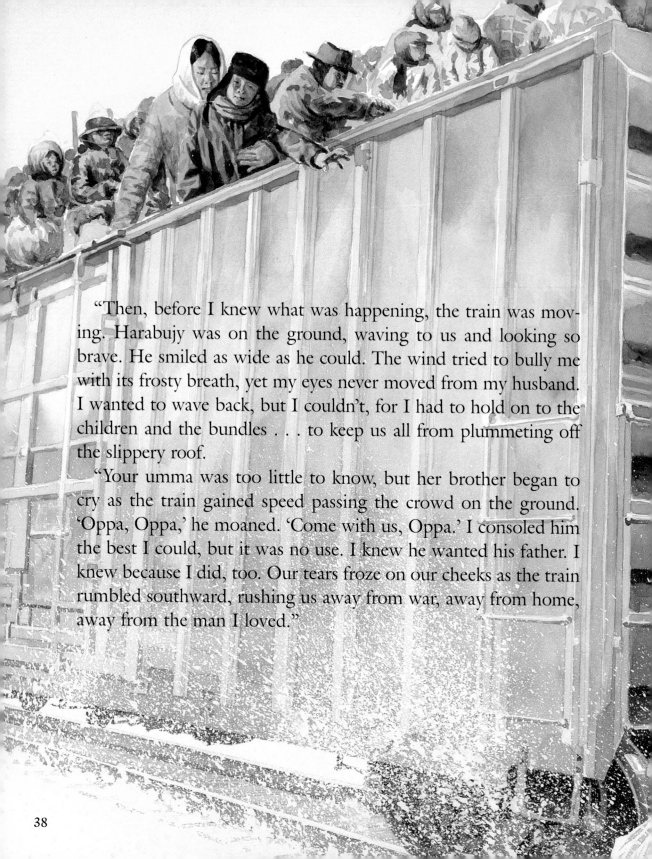

"Then, before I knew what was happening, the train was moving. Harabujy was on the ground, waving to us and looking so brave. He smiled as wide as he could. The wind tried to bully me with its frosty breath, yet my eyes never moved from my husband. I wanted to wave back, but I couldn't, for I had to hold on to the children and the bundles . . . to keep us all from plummeting off the slippery roof.

"Your umma was too little to know, but her brother began to cry as the train gained speed passing the crowd on the ground. 'Oppa, Oppa,' he moaned. 'Come with us, Oppa.' I consoled him the best I could, but it was no use. I knew he wanted his father. I knew because I did, too. Our tears froze on our cheeks as the train rumbled southward, rushing us away from war, away from home, away from the man I loved."

VII

I REACH WITH THE COOL CLOTH to wipe Harmuny's tears from her cheeks, just as she'd done for me earlier. "Tell me about the train ride, Harmuny. Did you make it to Pusan?"

Harmuny nods slowly. "Yes . . . but the journey was long. It was sad to see so many deserted farm fields and rice paddies. War had intruded on everyone's life, it seemed. The people we did see were all southbound, like us. Old people with tired bones and crooked canes did their best to keep up with their children and grandchildren. Those dogs not left behind panted alongside their exhausted masters.

"Young girls clutched bright folded blankets to their bosoms, and their brothers carried lumpy bundles in their skinny arms. Some people pushed carts, others pulled wagons. Most carried satchels and water canteens. Several times I saw young men sprint to grab on to the train, hoping for a ride, a chance for a brief rest.

"Those on the roof found it impossible to rest. Your umma was still a baby, so she wailed loudly throughout much of the trip. And her big brother fidgeted about, as young boys do. People complained. Room was scarce, and those without children resented the discomfort they caused. But I held my head high.

"When we saw sea gulls circle the skies, we knew we were approaching Pusan. After we left the train, the children and I found shelter in a school building. We met old neighbors and friends there, from Seoul."

Harmuny chuckles, remembering. "The local boys taught your uncle how to fish and dig for clams. Once he was pinched by a crab. But he didn't cry. He wanted to be brave, like his father."

Suddenly a light goes out of Harmuny's eyes, like a candle flickering dark. Her voice faint, she says, "And every time the soldiers came through, I searched their faces for Harabujy's." A whisper of a sigh flutters through her, and her small body seems to sag. "But I never found him. No, I never did."

VIII

SUDDENLY, FROM FAR BELOW, the blast of a train whistle echoes against the walls of the valley. *TWHOOOOOT, TWHOOOOOT!* it shrills as the cars thunder across the bridge, racing west as if to chase the setting sun.

Harmuny wraps me into the warmth of her shawl and we watch, both of us quiet. As my eyes follow the train, my mind drifts to Harabujy, who lost his life in the war all those years ago. I think about how his heart must have ached on that icy winter morning when he watched a peacebound train carry his family away from war, and away from him.

Then I think about Umma, who will be coming home to me one day. I think about the hug I will give her and the way her hand will feel, soft and warm in mine. I think about how I won't let her go, not for a long, long time.

Harmuny's raspy cough as she clears her throat draws me out of my thoughts. "Someday soon, Sumi, you and I will go down this hill to meet a train of our own," she says, her eyes blazing with faith. "We will be in that station and hear that whistle up close. You just wait and see."

I smile. "The train will be so loud, we'll have to plug our ears with cotton," I tell her, wishing I could hear it now.

Harmuny's eyes are glistening like stars. "But it won't matter a bit, because when that train screeches to a halt, and the conductor opens those doors . . ."

"Umma will step out," I finish for her, my spirit soaring at the thought. "Umma will be home."

"Safe and sound," whispers Harmuny, drawing me close.

"Safe and sound," I agree.

With Harmuny's arms around me, I press Umma's doll over my heart and listen as the wind scatters the last wistful echoes of the train whistle up to the twilight sky.

Author's Note

Although the characters in the book are fictional, they were inspired by real people, and real events.

On June 25, 1950, North Korean Communist troops invaded non-Communist South Korea. The following winter, the roof of a peacebound train carried my grandmother, Kim Chun Som, and her three young children (one of whom was my mother) to safety. Like the family in the book, they found shelter in the southeastern coastal city of Pusan. And though they suffered great hardships, they were among the lucky ones.

Some one million South Korean civilians were killed in the war. Another two and one-half million lost their homes. My grandfather, Dō Song Ho, was captured by the North Korean Communists early in the war. He was an electrical engineer, and like most other "professionals" who were seized by the enemy, he was never heard from again.

Neither side *won* the Korean War. Instead, a cease-fire was negotiated, and formally achieved on July 27, 1953. After the war, American troops remained in South Korea to ensure peace and helped South Koreans reconstruct their war-torn country. Four decades later South Korea continues to thrive, but many war survivors and descendants fear that, with neighboring North Korea still a Communist nation, there may someday be another invasion . . . and another Korean War.

Korean Words Used in This Book

harabujy	HAH' rah buh jee	grandfather
harmuny	HAR' muh nee	grandmother
oppa	OP'pah	informal word for father: "dad"
Pusan	BOO' sahn (Korean pronunciation)	a Korean city located on the southeastern coast of the Korean Peninsula
Seoul	SUH' oor (Korean pronunciation)	capital city of South Korea, located in the central region of the Korean Peninsula
umma	UM' ma	informal word for mother: "mom"
yuh-bo	YUH' bo	a term of endearment husbands and wives use for each other